Why Can't I Fly?

For Ruth

Why Can't I Fly?

Ken Brown

Ⓐ

Andersen Press · London

Early one morning, all the animals were gathered, as usual, by the water.
"I wish I could fly," thought the Ostrich. "Why can't I fly?" he asked the Sparrow.

"Maybe your neck is too long," suggested the Sparrow. "The flamingoes have long necks and they can fly," replied the Ostrich, "so why can't I?"

"I don't know," chirped the Sparrow, "perhaps your legs are too long."
"The storks have long legs and they can fly," said the Ostrich, "so why can't I?"

"Well perhaps your wings are too small," said the Sparrow.
"You've got small wings and you can fly," answered the
Ostrich, "so why can't I?"
"Well, I don't know! Maybe you just don't try hard
enough," and so saying the Sparrow flew away.

"Try hard enough indeed!" thought the Ostrich. "I'll show him.

I'll show all of them that I can fly."

So he ran as fast as he could

and, flapping his wings, he jumped off a high sand dune…

only to land, seconds later, with a terrible thud.

Next he climbed to the top of a huge rock.
"I'll show them!" he panted.
With his wings flailing the air, he threw himself over
the edge, but instantly plunged downwards and landed
headfirst in the soft sand below.

He remained with his head in the sand, too
embarrassed to show his face.
"I'll show them!" he thought." If my wings are too
small, I'll make them bigger."
Using some large leaves, bamboo canes, strong vines
and a great deal of skill, he constructed a flying machine.

Then he climbed to the top of the high rock again, and launched himself into the air.
"This is it! Look at me, everyone. I'm flying," cried the Ostrich.

But he spoke too soon! Moments later he landed with an almighty splash right in the middle of the river. "Never mind," said the Sparrow. "Your long neck will keep your head well above water!"

But the Ostrich was not put off by this, his first
disastrous attempt at flying. He built another flying
machine with even bigger wings and once again
launched himself into the air.
"Out of my way!" he shouted to the doves. "Out of my
way – I'm flying!"

Alas, this flight also ended in complete disaster, when the Ostrich became totally entangled in the leaves of a high palm tree.

"Never mind!" chirped the Sparrow. "Your long legs will certainly help you to get down from there."

The Ostrich, however, was just as determined as ever to fly; he would not give up. So he built an even bigger flying machine and for the third time climbed to the top of the high rock. He took a deep breath and launched himself yet again into the air. This time, instead of plummeting straight downwards as before, he soared high up into the sky, as gracefully as any other bird. "Look at me!" shouted the triumphant Ostrich. "Look, everybody, I'm flying!" But the only reply that he got was the sound of his own voice echoing about the empty skies.

The Ostrich couldn't understand it!

"Where is everyone?" he cried. "Where's Sparrow? I'm flying and there's no one here to see. They'll never believe me now."

But they did!

More Andersen Press paperback picture books!

MICHAEL
by Tony Bradman and Tony Ross

THE SANDAL
by Tony Bradman and Philippe Dupasquier

OUR PUPPY'S HOLIDAY
by Ruth Brown

NOTHING BUT TROUBLE
by Gus Clarke

FRIGHTENED FRED
by Peta Coplans

THE PERFECT PET
by Peta Coplans

A SUNDAY WITH GRANDPA
by Philippe Dupasquier

I'LL TAKE YOU TO MRS COLE
by Nigel Gray and Michael Foreman

WHAT'S INSIDE?
by Satoshi Kitamura

THERE'S A HOLE IN MY BUCKET
by Ingrid and Dieter Schubert

A LITTLE BIT OF WINTER
by Paul Stuart and Chris Riddell

ELEPHANT AND CROCODILE
by Max Velthuijs